# NIGHT OF THE RIDER
# BY ALYSON FAYE

# A SHORT SHARP SHOCKS!
# BOOK

# BOOK: 18

COPYRIGHT INFORMATION



For further information, please visit:

WEB: www.demainpublishing.com
TWITTER: @DemainPubUk
FACEBOOK: Demain Publishing
INSTAGRAM: demainpublishing

# CONTENTS

# NIGHT OF THE RIDER

The brambles tore at Barnabas' bare skin; the wood rustled and murmured and roots tripped him whilst animals paused in mid-forage, faces lifted, sniffing his fear-soaked sweat. In a break amidst the line of beeches Barnabas glimpsed a sickly light.

"Thank God," he wheezed. His ribs ached. He was certain he'd cracked one in the last tumble he'd taken. The turrets of Milner House stretched craggy stone fingers towards the night sky. Barnabas' heart pounded. "Home! So close."

The wind picked up and on its breath he heard a distant horn blowing. "The dogs! They're coming! Open the damn door!" He lunged across the moon-dappled ornamental lawns. A nymph perching beside a fountain snickered and gushed water from stone lips. Barnabas heard a volley of howls. Behind him hooves detonated the undergrowth.

Glancing over his shoulder, blood seeping through his shirt, Barnabas wished he'd never accepted the hunchback's tainted money, wished he'd walked away from the gambling tables and thrown away his beloved dice.

The Rider broke through the tree line; a massive silhouette atop a coal black horse. "Halt prey!"

The words echoed through Barnabas' skull, although the Rider had no lips with which to form speech. Instead Barnabas sensed the Rider's thoughts. Pain spiked at his temples. If, at that moment, Barnabas had a mirror to glance in, he would have observed spiders' webs of broken blood vessels flooding his corneas.

A fox screamed in the woods; an aperitif for the hounds, starving and primed for the kill. A rangy figure loomed before the oak door of Milner House, carrying in the crook of his elbow, a bulky shot bow.

"Faster lad!" his father's familiar voice urged him on as when he'd been a child running after a ball in play. This was no game though.

Barnabas sobbed, choked and using his last breaths, pushed his body onwards. His broken ribs burned. He could discern the hounds' panting, their excited whimpering. A bolt from his father's crossbow flew past his head; its wind chafed his cheeks. The missile flew true, found its target and behind him a dog yelped, then fell silent.

The Rider's fury overwhelmed Barnabas' senses. A wave of dissonance swept across the lawns. Myriad statues cracked and the fountain's waters bubbled. Blood flowed from Barnabas' nose and ears, but he paid it no heed. *Only the dead don't bleed*, he thought. *Push on. I can make it.*

A second bolt rushed past his cheek, followed by another hound's anguished cry.

"Father!" Barnabas lurched across the threshold. The door clanged shut. Father and son stood staring at each other. Faces equally grim.

"Will it hold?" Barnabas stared at the five-centuries old wood.

His father shrugged. "We'll find out. What have you done to fetch out the Rider and the Hunt? Something ill-advised, I warrant."

Barnabas collapsed on to the stone flags. "I couldn't pay, Pa. I lost it all. I am sorry." Behind his shoulders the door's wood throbbed and thrummed, as though under assault. But it held.

"The Rider never forgets. He has your scent. No one outruns him and his hounds. You know as much, lad." His father turned away, shoulders slumped. Sorrow etched in every gesture. "You can rest here for a few days, but you cannot stay longer. You have marked us and placed this whole household and your sister in danger."

Barnabas lay face down on the stone flags, riven with pain and humiliation, watching his father's boots march away from him. He was alone. Or so he believed.

Beyond the grounds of Milner House, on the borders of the land, the Rider bided his time, masked by the trees' foliage. His surviving quartet of hounds lay awaiting his instructions.

His antlered helmet, soldered centuries ago, scraped the lower branches. The iron visor shrouded his face, except for his eyes, whose irises were golden as a hawk's; they perceived what mortal men never could: every scurrying animal in the woods, every bird's nest and every human's footfall.

The lad should never have escaped him. It was hardly possible. Yet it had happened. Tugging on the black, leather reins, the Rider turned his horse's head around and one by one the hounds stood up, stretched and galloped after their master.

Noses to the earth, ears flopping, tails tucked down.

Sorrow-struck.

***

Above Barnabas, on the landing, his sister Leonie kept watch; disguised by the shadows, in her usual hidey spot. On the cusp of eighteen years of age and soon to be wed, she was eager to learn more about the Rider. In her eyes this cursed figure seemed far more fascinating than her husband-to-be. She had often listened to the village women chattering over their chores about the darkness at the heart of the Rider and what forces drove him.

"Barney, you goose," his sister murmured. "You've thrown away a glittering opportunity, all because of your foolish passion for cards."

She knew she would not have behaved in the same way. Leonie was old beyond her years, being motherless from such a young age and raised in a household of men, had led her to develop an inner life filled with secrets.

She had heard the thundering horse's hooves come ever closer to the house. She'd been out of bed in a moment, heart thumping, dashing to the casement window and kneeling behind the velvet drapes, desperate to spy on the scene below.

From that vantage spot she had watched her older brother race across the lawn, his shirt flying behind him, glimpsed the hounds at his heels and behind the pack, a mammoth figure, astride a horse, helmeted, with horns reaching to the night sky—the Rider. He was taller than the tallest man in the village, broader in the chest and exuding a force which shattered the statues in his path.

"A glimpse of his golden eyes is all it takes for a maiden to fall." The village women used to say with a wink between themselves.

"Look up. Oh please, look up at me," Leonie begged and, to her amazed joy, the helmeted head paused, sniffed the air and did look up towards her bedroom window. The Rider's gaze seemed to fix her face on his retinas—her hair blowing in the breeze, her rosy cheeks and her parted lips. His eyes held hers. The cursed, lost man within the Rider reached out and Leonie answered. Though no words were spoken. There was a communion.

When she peeked over the sill once again, the only signs of the Rider's visit were the shattered stones splayed across the lawn. The forest had swallowed him whole.

***

Leonie cornered her brother after supper in the study, where he was relaxing supping brandy, his ribs freshly strapped and bandaged. The alcohol dulling the pain and his fear.

"Tell me please, Barney, what is the big city like? Is it true a woman can be as free as a man there and she doesn't have to wear corsets? You can love whomever you wish?"

Barnabas laughed at his sister's wide-eyed face and glowing cheeks. He knew he should reprimand her for not being in her bedroom asleep, but in truth he wanted company. Despair ate at him. He patted the stool by his knee for her to perch upon and Leonie nestled against him.

*How sweet and lovely she is*, he thought tenderly. Warm affection replaced the pain, mixing with the brandy; a drug to his damaged pride and body.

"No. What rot you talk, Leonie! Women marry whomever their fathers tell them to or else they are thrown out on to the streets, which I can promise you are not paved with gold, to become nothing but common ..."—he lowered his voice to a whisper—"whores."

Leonie perked up at the illicit word. "Have you met any...whores, Barney?" She too whispered the word and glanced at the door to ensure her father was not hovering in earshot.

"One or two," her brother muttered, frowning. "In fact, that's why I ended up..." he trailed off, staring gloomy-faced into the fire.

Leonie wriggled closer, resting her right cheek against Barnabas' thigh. "Do tell, Barney." She used his childhood nickname deliberately. He was five years older than her and she'd adored him as a child, following him everywhere, until it was deemed unsuitable for her to do so and the tedious lessons in how to be a lady began.

Barnabas' mouth took on a firm line. "No. No more idle chat, sweet sister." There was a pause, whilst the logs crackled under the onslaught of the flames. "When is your marriage day?"

"The summer solstice," Leonie announced, all trace of light and joy vanishing from her face.

Barnabas noticing, shook his head. "Jacob Hardcastle is a solid man from excellent stock."

Leonie shrugged. "He is old."

Barnabas laughed, "He is barely thirty years old, if that. His family is well to do. He can provide you with a comfortable home and life, Leonie. These are important matters."

Leonie gazed around at the heavy oak furniture, the wooden wall panelling and the glowering gazes of the family portraits—many bewhiskered and to her eyes, brimming with disapproval.

*How depressing 'well to do' is*. Resentful thoughts surged through her. "Tell me, why is the Rider hunting you?" She waited, fingers crossed, hoping Barnabas would leak some more secrets.

Her brother touched his ribs. "I made a…mistake, Leonie. Accepted a bet…I couldn't…wouldn't pay. But I've learned my lesson. It's the end of my gambling days. I promise you."

Leonie had heard this particular promise oft times, so she remained unimpressed. However, shrewdly she stroked his hand and pushed for more details. "They say the Rider has powers no human man has. They say he lived as a man once, but was altered by *darke magicke* and betrayed by the woman he loved. They say he is doomed to ride for eternity with his hounds or until the curse is broken." Her cheeks were flushed rosy pink. Her lips were slightly open.

Barnabas snorted. "Who has been telling you such nonsense, Leonie? Is this women's idle gossip? From the village?"

Leonie pouted, which had the effect of turning her pretty face sulky and doll-like. "He made you bleed from your nose and ears. I saw it, last night."

Barnabas brushed off her hand. Furious now, he stood up, remembering the intense pulsing power swamping his mind and smashing the garden statuary around him.

"Little baby sister, you ask too many questions. Time for bed." He patted her blonde hair absent-mindedly and pushed her away, albeit gently.

Reluctant, but knowing their shared intimacy to have evaporated, Leonie gathered her taffeta dressing gown around her and left Barnabas alone. He remained by the fire, deep in his thoughts. Recalling the sequence of events which had caused his downfall into debt and debauchery in London and led the Rider to his family's door.

"I was a fool," he whispered and flung his glass at the fireplace. It did not make Barnabas feel any better. Nothing would.

He was doomed to die.

No one could save him.

He knew that.

It was just a matter of days.

***

London! God what a magical, fascinating city it had appeared to his eyes. A young man fresh from the bucolic countryside, sporting a thick brogue, heavy whiskers and a bulging wallet. Soho was his choice of location for his digs and he spent his days drinking and gambling with a crowd he knew his father would never allow over the threshold at home.

Amongst Barnabas' hedonistic circle were a few who fancied themselves artistic—who painted, wrote poetry and visited the theatre. How Barnabas adored the glamour of the shows; the songs with their witty, filthy lyrics, the wine which flowed and the girls who fluttered around him like vivid, glorious dragonflies.

One in particular, Marie, who danced nightly in the chorus, caught his roving eye. Vibrant, with waist-length red hair and shapely legs, which she exposed to advantage in the brief costumes she wore on stage. Night after night Barnabas watched her frolic on the boards then together they frolicked till dawn, in and out of his bed. His money flowed like wine and whiskey. Rivers of the wonderful stuff.

Until the day it stopped—dead. Dammed at the source. His father cut him off with no notice. Barnabas pleaded, begged, wrote letters—but to no avail. His father stood firm. Barnabas slid swiftly into debt and Marie, he discovered, had expectations of a certain lifestyle, trimmed with clothes, shoes, meals and pretty geegaws. By then Barnabas loved her or at least he believed he did.

Barnabas' face soured at the memory. He briefly wondered where Marie was now? And with which fool? He didn't flatter himself she would be alone, crying over his departure. Not her.

"Course I love yer, darlin'," she crooned, sitting on his knee and fiddling with her hair, all the while kissing him. "But I've got expenses too—dressmaker, wigs, shoes. It all adds up when you're a stage star, like moi."

Marie fancied herself part French, but it was just a fantasy. As was her claim to be a star, for in reality she had 'chorus' stamped all over her.

Barnabas remembered how for a brief, blissful spell he'd had a winning streak at the cards and dice—but that's how you are drawn in, he'd realised later. Next they ensure you lose, huge amounts—more than you could ever win back.

Night after night he returned, hooked, wriggling, strangling under the weight of the mounting debts. He wrote promissory notes by the handful, till he owed thousands and thousands of pounds. In desperation he pawned nearly everything he owned.

One night, caught between his landlord's violence and the debt collectors' waiting fists, he'd done a bunk into the squalid alleyways of the city, sleeping in a piss-drenched doorway next to an undertaker's premises. The irony of this being possibly the last stop for him, did not go amiss.

So he turned to Marie, the love of his life, for assistance. "I have a friend," she confided. "He can help you, sweetheart. Trust me." Fool that he was, he'd taken her at her word.

The 'friend' turned out to be a twisted, hunchback fellow with a sallow tint to his flesh. He lent Barney oodles of money, at first with smiles, but a few weeks later when it was apparent there was no chance of repayment, he offered Barnabas a new deal.

Barney shuddered at the memory. It still sickened him. He could not face the pain of the procedure or what it would mean for him. At first he'd thought it was a joke, in poor taste, but still a jest.

"Just let us take your teeth, sir. Yes, the whole mouthful. I have a client, rich, elderly. We could fashion the most desirable dental plate with your strong white teeth. Here, allow me to look inside."

The hunchback levered Barney's lips open with a spatula and peered inside. Counting his molars and incisors, he wrote down the numbers in his accounts ledger. "Yes, that should clear the debt satisfactorily."

"You're jesting, sir." Barney pulled away from the hunchback's questing fingers. "I'd be eating slop for the rest of my life. I'd be an old man with a withered mouth before I was twenty-five."

*Worse still*, he thought, *no decent lass would ever kiss me again. My courting days would be done for.*

"Better to be old than dead, my friend," the hunchback responded and extracted a pair of bloodstained pliers from his leather apron pocket. He waved them in Barney's face, as if taunting him.

Acting on instinct, Barney punched the hunchback full in the face. The man fell back and his skull cracked on the stone table's lip, where the ledgers lay. Barney fled, not waiting to check if the grotesque freak still drew breath or not.

Returning to his newer, dingier lodgings, Barnabas learned Marie had stolen the two remaining items of value he'd kept hold of—his father's eighteenth birthday-gift, a gold pocket watch and his mother's silver picture frame. His mother's image lay on the carpet, ripped in half, staring up at him as if to say, "I warned you Barney, I tried."

He sat on the thin carpet, tears falling. He believed nothing worse could happen to him, but within a few days, he discovered this was far from the truth. However, calamitous the situation appeared, it could always get worse.

In his desperation Barnabas had overlooked the evidence of the hunchback's foul trade. He'd chosen to ignore the contents of the bottles arranged on the shelves; the grisly remnants of illegal surgeries—the floating body parts, unwanted foetuses, varied internal organs Barney didn't know the name of. He preferred such things to remain unnamed. The hunchback sold his trophies to a network of rich, powerful clients. God knows, well in all likelihood the Devil knew, what these wealthy buyers did with them thereafter.

It was one of these well-connected but less than upright gentlemen who passed on Barnabas' name and varied items of his clothing, acquired from the pawn shops, all carrying his scent to those in the countryside who could for coin, contact the Rider.

A whisper in London, a rumour in the towns beyond, but in the countryside and the forested areas, the Rider was myth come to life. No one who worked the land or lived in a remote village doubted for one moment he was real. His horn's woeful notes filled the nights, his hounds' baying followed after and if you were unfortunate enough to linger too close—you would feel the massive black horse's hooves at your heels.

Out of options, Barney fled from London, hoping his father's distant, lonely country house would provide him with sanctuary. He would rather be dead however, than share this sordid, sorry tale with his sweet, untouched sister.

He had to protect her.

It was his role.

***

The Rider retreated into the night-time camouflage offered by the forest. This was his domain. His senses heightened by the long-ago loss of his speech, scented every animal's spoor. His hawk's vision discerned every movement around him. He wore the darkness like a cloak; a familiar friend. His only friend.

He experienced few defeats. The lad's last-minute flight to safety thus being a rare occurrence. Prey, once targeted, became dead meat for his hounds within hours. Barnabas carried the charm of the truly blessed; however the Rider knew it was a temporary setback.

Dismounting, he tethered his horse and built a camp-fire, before skinning and cooking a rabbit. Not for his evening repast, but for the hounds. The dogs should, by rights, have feasted on the lad's spilled guts but it had been denied them. They were restless, frustrated and unwilling to settle at his side. They missed their slain brethren; the pair felled by the bolts.

The Rider unstrapped his helmet, allowing himself a rare opportunity to relax. The iron helmet dropped to his side, the antlers scraping patterns in the dirt. The hounds stared at the face of their master—silenced. Tails and ears lowered in terror, at what they saw.

It had been many generations since the Rider had lived and breathed as a man. The centuries of *darke magicke* had warped and distorted his features beyond recognition. He had no use for mirrors and no desire to look upon his visage. The cursed do not need to see the evidence of their damnation.

Once, many seasons ago, he had been handsome, in the prime of life, with thick hair the colour of chestnuts and eyes just as brown. Now his scalp was bald, the hair eroded by the pressure of the helmet and his eyes rested sunken in their sockets. His nose had collapsed inwards and to ensure he could never plead for help or tell his tale, his mouth and lips had been removed, leaving a tight, shiny carapace of skin in their place. His flesh was the colour of a dying candle—waxy and curdled.

He stripped off his weaponry, the metal-linked shirt, his heavy gloves, revealing hands, brutal in strength and capable of ripping a rabbit in half. Great fortitude, stamina and endurance had been gifted to him. He could ride for days without rest. It was his curse.

Across his chest an elaborate pattern had been burned into his flesh. A tattoo of intertwining shapes, diamonds and pentagons overlaid each other. It was precise and elaborate, but it was also the mark of ownership. He belonged body and soul to *the darke* to do with as they pleased.

He lay down upon his wolves' skin cloak, whilst one of the youngest, most foolhardy of the hounds, hardly more than a puppy herself, slunk to his side to nestle against him. The older dogs observed, waiting for the whack of the hand slamming away the intruder. It did not come. The Rider touched the pup's head, stroked her soft velvet ears then put his hand around her furry torso. Master and pup slept.

In his dreams the Rider lived out his first life; his human life. He revisited his village, his wife, his children, the smithy where he'd worked and finally the mistress he'd seduced in a moment of drunken lust. The next morning, sober and regretful he had rejected her and she had sworn vengeance upon him. He'd had the arrogance to laugh at her. What a fool he had been!

She'd hissed, spat in his face. "Do you know with whom you meddle, blacksmith?"

Laughing, he had named and shamed her. "Yes, I meddle with you and I do not care to any longer than I have. Whore!"

Outside the sky blackened, though it was barely midday, the air turned as thick and hot as the steam coming off his anvil and all the while her lips spat words at him, which he did not understand, but he guessed were ancient. Perhaps even from the days when dragons roamed the land. Then in front of him, in a whirlwind of dust and wind, she vanished.

He'd searched for her for days, to plead for forgiveness and to offer to make amends in any way he could—with gold or the human child she had begged him for during their one shared night. He could not find her. She had disappeared and no one in the surrounding villages had glimpsed her passing their way.

It was as if she had never existed. But he knew different, for he had kissed her all through that one blasted night and his treacherous lips were rotting now under the power of her spell.

The changes came slowly over the next few months. For a short period, he was able to hide them but when his mutation became too obvious, he holed up indoors, wrapped in blankets, venturing out only under cover of darkness.

He heard the villagers' whispers and understood their fear. He knew he did not have many days before they came for him and when they did he guessed, in their blood-lust, they would slaughter his family. Thalia, his wife, tried to stay loyal to him, but he didn't blame her for finally breaking down and fleeing from his wrecked, stinking body. He disgusted himself. He was an aberration.

One night in mid-summer he took his blackest, sleekest horse and rode away. He vowed to ride the length and breadth of the land searching for his mistress, searching for her absolution. He would beg on his knees before her.

It had been so long ago, so many generations had been born and since died. His children had birthed their own families many times over and still he was compelled to ride and hunt. There was no forgiveness for him to be found anywhere.

The Rider stirred in his sleep, a single tear fell from his eye onto the pup's charcoal fur.

The pup snuffled and turned over, displaying her pink stomach to the trees' unseeing gaze.

***

Leonie lay sprawled in her bedroom on the third floor, directly above Barnabas still brooding in the study, on her duck-feather elderdown, leafing through the pages of a miniature book. She had retrieved it from under the floorboards, where she kept her cache of forbidden materials bought or traded from the village's womenfolk and from the markets, where she regularly sought out the unusual, the weird and the magical.

Raised with her father acting as both parents and her brother being her only surviving sibling, she missed a mother's guiding hand. There had been a sad string of dead babies or stillbirths, but she did not remember them nor did she remember her mother, who had swiftly followed the last dead babe into the grave, before Leonie celebrated her third birthday.

Perhaps a mother might have tamed Leonie's interests and energy; encouraged her to walk a more traditional and safer path. Left to her own devices, Leonie explored far and wide in her reading, her activities and her leisure interests. Her father, too occupied by his own business activities, proved unable to supervise her every hour of the day and night.

She had been escaping from Milner House after dark since she'd been eight years old, roaming the woods collecting animal bones, feathers, quartz, ferns and frog spawn. All of which she was adept at hiding from the adults' sight.

The miniature book represented her most precious possession. She remembered how the dark skinned merchant swore it was fashioned from human skin, with the spells inscribed in human blood. The handwriting was looping and faded to a pale rust, so his story could be true. Leonie loved to stroke the cover, wondering who had worn the skin? A child perhaps? A puny, sickly baby? Like the ones her mother had lost.

Leonie muttered the twisting, complicated syllables of the spells, trying to get as close to the exact pronunciation as she could. Accuracy mattered, or so the merchant had told her. As did the use of blood in the ritual. Her own.

From under her mattress, Leonie extracted the elegant kitchen knife she had stolen earlier that evening. *If it can slice a whole chicken, it can cut me easily.* The thought gave her power.

Holding the handle in her left hand she pressed the blade firmly on to her right wrist, aiming for the centre of the blue tracery of veins. A weedy trickle of liquid dribbled out, tears sprang to her eyes and sweat beaded her brow. She gasped with the pain, but bit her lip and kept pressing down. This was harder than she had anticipated. The drops which fell on to the vellum of the book were instantly absorbed and this encouraged her.

She kept reciting the peculiar, ugly phrases of the magic words, which though they meant nothing to her, she prayed held some power of their own. After a few minutes her blood flowed more freely and Leonie let it drip onto her nightgown and the carpet. Her vision kept blurring and waves of dizziness engulfed her.

Outside Milner House the wind rose, tossing the branches around, scratching at the windows as if begging for entry. Absorbed in her spell-making, Leonie did not notice.

However, less than two miles away someone else's attention had been snared.

***

Lured from his slumbers beside the ebbing embers of the camp fire, the Rider lifted his antlered head and sniffed the air. Blood. Willingly offered. He could smell desire. A woman's. His gold eyes flickered and where his lips had once been, the shiny skin twitched into the simulacrum of a smile. In his chest flickered something new, he'd not felt in hundreds of years: hope.

"*I am coming*," the Rider telegraphed his thoughts and the silent syllables winged their way through the trees over the immaculate lawns up to Leonie's bedroom.

She received the message, hearing it in her head with a fluttering of excitement in the pit of her stomach. The blood flowed lavishly now from her left wrist. The deeper the cuts proving the most efficient. Increasing faintness was dragging her under though.

"Hurry," she whispered. Leonie collapsed on to her lacy pillows, oblivious to the blood staining the French bed linen.

Barnabas, still pondering his own troubles, did not notice anything amiss until a shutter banged against the outside wall. When he rose to latch it, he noted how the treetops tossed wildly. Sniffing, he smelt the air charging with a strange energy. He did not know how to describe it. But it tasted tangy, coppery and salty. He licked his lips in puzzlement. Then he understood.

"Lock all the doors!" he yelled, running through the house. "Shutter the windows! The Rider is coming."

The servants flurried and flocked about, obeying the young master's instructions, confused but loyal. No one doubted his word. He had escaped the Rider once, which was a miracle, so the young master knew better than anyone who and what was coming.

The horn blew one pure note and everyone inside Milner House froze in mid-action.

"He's close!" shrieked the housemaid and promptly fainted, overwhelmed by the circumstances she found herself in. The Cook and Butler carried her, between them, to the kitchen and bolted themselves inside. Cook extinguished all the lights and clutching a carving knife and a Bible, hoped she had every eventuality covered.

The baying of the hounds carried through the night air. The moon appeared from behind a cloud and Barnabas glimpsed the mighty horse with its Rider standing on the lawn. He cast no moon shadow, but around him and his mount, the fountain churned and the grass turned black and withered.

"*Come and face me*," the Rider's instructions sang inside Barnabas' skull.

Behind him Barnabas heard his father's steady tread, then felt his warm hand on his shoulder. "Stay lad. Do not venture out there."

Barnabas had never known such fear in his life, not even when facing the tooth pulling hunchback. Waiting outside, was no human sinner, but something created by darkness and it had no conscience or compassion. You could not reason with it or bargain. It followed its own rules.

A crack appeared in the parlour windows, Barnabas watched it creep downwards then shatter into a spider's web. Above his head a window banged open and he heard, to his horror, a voice he knew well.

"I am here, Rider. Come for me. I am waiting."

Father and son gazed at each in dread. "Leonie, no!" Barnabas raced for the stairs, leaping them in threes and pushing open the door to his sister's bedroom.

The sight which greeted him, so appalled him he froze, mouth open in horror.

He sensed his father close at his heels.

His darling sister lay in a widening pool of blood turning her nightgown claret and her bed sheets crimson. Her blonde hair spread wild and tangled on her pillow, her lips were turning blue, but she still breathed. Her voice, though frail, was audible.

"I will not marry whom you choose, father. I choose another. If he will have me. If I have given enough of my life force for him." A knife rested at her side, whilst etched in the flesh of her left arm, a gaping wound stretched from elbow to wrist.

Behind him their father cried out, "Leonie, what have you done to yourself, child?" He rushed to her bedside, weeping.

The Rider pronounced, *She is mine."*

Barnabas sensed a presence behind him at the window. Turning he came face to face with the antlered helmet and the golden eyes of myth and legend. The figure of the Rider hovered, floating above his horse's saddle, with his cloak unfurling in the air, resembling nothing so much as a huge bird of prey. It was the stuff of nightmare. Around his body the air fizzed with sparks; a blue halo outlined his entire figure.

Barnabas' father, clutching the iron bedstead frame at Leonie's side, cried out in pain as blue sparks flew across the room and Barnabas heard a thud as his father's body hit the carpet.

Then silence.

Barnabas could not move his head. The Rider would not let him. In the golden depths he saw obsidian flecks rotating and beyond them he glimpsed a lifetime of hell. Barnabas' skin began to crawl, as though millions of ants were running over him, his nose and ears leaked blood, his mouth dried up, his bladder opened and yet still, he could not move away.

Leonie whispered, "Let him go, Rider. I choose to come with you. Free him. He is of my flesh."

Barnabas collapsed like a broken marionette to the floor, lying in his own puddle of piss, crying and scratching at his skin.

The Rider stretched out his gloved hands and Leonie staggered, tiny step by tiny step to the windowsill and there he lifted her, cradling her body as if she were made of gold and diamonds. He lowered his antlered head and rested it upon her blonde hair, sharing her breaths and taking them into his lungs.

Leonie's breathing strengthened and the colour returned to her cheeks and blue lips. They were conjoined. His breath being hers. He stroked her gouged left arm and at his touch the blood dried, the flow dammed and the wound sealed over with a fine film.

Barnabas lying on the floor, gazed up astonished, at the sight of the death-bringer who was giving life back to his sister. Leonie reached up a hand and stroked the iron helmet with such tenderness, fresh tears sprang in Barnabas' eyes and in his sister's face was such rapture, he could hardly believe what he was seeing. She loved this monster, this cursed figure. How she could, he would never comprehend. But his younger, weaker, adored but rebellious sister had saved his life.

"Your debt is paid. You are the most fortunate of human men." The words thrummed inside his skull, hurting at first but then fading to a gentle hum. Barnabas staggered to his feet and stumbled to the window. He knew this would be his last chance to see Leonie again, in this life.

Together, as one, the Rider and Leonie dropped into the saddle. He carried her gently before him, propping her torso against his chest, before urging his horse into a canter. The strange couple rode away at a swift pace across the moonlit lawns towards the welcoming forest. The hounds galloped alongside, their tails upright.

All Barnabas could make out of his sister was her blonde, tousled head and her nightgown trailing blood-stained ribbons in her wake. Just before the trees swallowed them the Rider paused his mount and turned. Leonie raised her hand in a final farewell.

Her expression was one of bliss.

# **BIOGRAPHY**

Alyson lives in West Yorkshire with her husband, teen son and four rescue animals.

Her fiction has been published widely in print anthologies: DeadCades, Women in Horror Annual 2, Trembling with Fear 1 & 2, Coffin Bell Journal 1, Stories from Stone, Ellipsis, Rejected (ed. Erin Crocker) and in many ezines, but most often on the Horror Tree site, and in The Siren's Call.

In May 2019 *Night of the Rider*, was published by Demain in their Short Sharp Shocks! ebook series and later that year Demain published her 1940's crime novella, *Maggie Of My Heart*.

Currently she has stories due out in the Strange Girls anthology (ed. Azzurra Nox), a charity anthology, Burning Love from Things in the Well, and there is more to come from Black Hare Press and Gypsum Sound Press.

Her work has been read on podcasts (e.g. Ladies of Horror) and The Casket of Fictional Delights.

She performs at open mics, teaches, edits and hangs out with her dog on the moor in all weathers.

She enjoys swimming, crafting and singing.

For more information, please check out:
Twitter: @AlysonFaye2

https://alysonfayewordpress.wordpress.com/

https://www.amazon.co.uk/Alyson-Faye/e/B01NBYSLRT

https://www.ladiesofhorrorfiction.com/the-lohf-directory/profile-alyson-faye

# ADRIAN BALDWIN (COVER ARTIST)

Adrian is a Mancunian now living and working in Wales. Back in the 1990s, he wrote for various TV shows/personalities: Smith & Jones, Clive Anderson, Brian Conley, Paul McKenna, Hale & Pace, Rory Bremner (and a few others). Wooo, get him! Since then, he has written three screenplays—one of which received generous financial backing from the Film Agency for Wales. Then along came the global recession which kicked the UK Film industry in the nuts. What a bummer! Not to be outdone, he turned to novel writing—which had always been his real dream—and, in particular, a genre he feels is often overlooked; a genre he has always been a fan of: Dark Comedy (sometimes referred to as Horror's weird cousin). *Barnacle Brat* (a dark comedy for grown-ups), his first novel won Indie Novel of the Year 2016 award; his second novel *Stanley Mccloud Must Die!* (more dark comedy for grown-ups) published in 2016 and his third: *The Snowman And The Scarecrow* (another dark comedy for grown-ups) published in 2018. Adrian Baldwin has also written and published a number of dark comedy short stories. He designs book covers too—not just for his own books but for a growing number of publishers. For more information on the award-winning author, check out: https://adrianbaldwin.info/

# DEMAIN PUBLISHING

To keep up to-date on all news DEMAIN (including future submission calls and releases) you can follow us in a number of ways:

BLOG:
www.demainpublishingblog.weebly.com

TWITTER:
@DemainPubUk

FACEBOOK PAGE:
Demain Publishing

INSTAGRAM:
demainpublishing

Book 26: The Elixir – Lee Allen Howard
Book 27: Breaking The Habit – Yolanda Sfetsos
Book 28: Forfeit Tissue – C. C. Adams
Book 29: Crown Of Thorns – Trevor Kennedy
Book 30: The Encampment / Blood Memory – Zachary Ashford
Book 31: Dreams Of Lake Drukka / Exhumation – Mike Thorn
Book 32: Apples / Snail Trails – Russell Smeaton
Book 33: An Invitation To Darkness – Hailey Piper
Book 34: The Necessary Evils & Sick Girl – Dan Weatherer
Book 35: The Couvade – Joanna Koch
Book 36: The Camp Creeper & Other Stories – Dave Jeffery
Book 37: Flaying Sins – Ian Woodhead
Book 38: Hearts & Bones – Theresa Derwin
Book 39: The Unbeliever & The Intruder – Morgan K. Tanner
Book 40: The Coffin Walk – Richard Farren Barber
Book 41: The Straitjacket In The Woods – Kitty R. Kane
Book 42: Heart Of Stone – M. Brandon Robbins
Book 43: Bits – R.A. Busby
Book 44: Last Meal In Osaka & Other Stories – Gary Buller
Book 45: The One That Knows No Fear – Steve Stred
Book 46: The Birthday Girl & Other Stories – Christopher Beck
Book 47: Crowded House & Other Stories  - S.J. Budd
Book 48: Hand To Mouth – Deborah Sheldon
Book 49: Moonlight Gunshot Mallet Flame / A Little Death – Alicia Hilton
Book 50: Dark Corners - David Charlesworth

# Murder! Mystery! Mayhem!

Maggie Of My Heart – Alyson Faye
The Funeral Birds – Paula R.C. Readman
Cursed – Paul M. Feeney

# Anthologies

The Darkest Battlefield – Tales Of WW1/Horror

# Horror Novellas

House Of Wrax – Raven Dane
A Quiet Apocalypse – Dave Jeffery

# General Fiction

Joe – Terry Grimwood
Finding Jericho – Dave Jeffery

# PRAISE FOR
# NIGHT OF THE RIDER

"A great story well told."
– Mari Phillips (via Amazon)

"Enthralling from the start."
– Mrs G. S. Wright (via Amazon)

"This spooky wild hunt is a great read!"
– Amazon Customer

"A stunning story, with rich atmospheric tones."
– Jenny Bookworm (via Amazon)

"This supernatural gothic tale hits every sweet spot!"
– Deborah Sheldon (via Goodreads)

"Fast pacing, great characters and a brilliant plot!"
– Paula R.C. Readman (via Goodreads)

"This was my first time reading Alyson Faye…it won't
be my last." – Michael (via Goodreads)

# DEMAIN PUBLISHING

## <u>Short Sharp Shocks!</u>

Book 0: Dirty Paws - Dean M. Drinkel
Book 1: Patient K - Barbie Wilde
Book 2: The Stranger & The Ribbon – Tim Dry
Book 3: Asylum Of Shadows – Stephanie Ellis
Book 4: Monster Beach – Ritchie Valentine Smith
Book 5: Beasties & Other Stories – Martin Richmond
Book 6: Every Moon Atrocious – Emile-Louis Tomas Jouvet
Book 7: A Monster Met – Liz Tuckwell
Book 8: The Intruders & Other Stories – Jason D. Brawn
Book 9: The Other – David Youngquist
Book 10: Symphony Of Blood – Leah Crowley
Book 11: Shattered – Anthony Watson
Book 12: The Devil's Portion – Benedict J. Jones
Book 13: Cinders Of A Blind Man Who Could See – Kev Harrison
Book 14: Dulce Et Decorum Est – Dan Howarth
Book 15: Blood, Bears & Dolls – Allison Weir
Book 16: The Forest Is Hungry – Chris Stanley
Book 17: The Town That Feared Dusk – Calvin Demmer
Book 18: Night Of The Rider – Alyson Faye
Book 19: Isidora's Pawn – Erik Hofstatter
Book 20: Plain – D.T. Griffith
Book 21: Supermassive Black Mass – Matthew Davis
Book 22: Whispers Of The Sea (& Other Stories) – L. R. Bonehill
Book 23: Magic – Eric Nash
Book 24: The Plague – R.J. Meldrum
Book 25: Candy Corn – Kevin M. Folliard